VLAD
THE WORLD'S
WORST
VAMPIRE

Spook-tacular Surprise

ANNA WILSON
ILLUSTRATED BY
KATHRYN DURST

Stripes

The sun was setting over Misery Manor.
It was Sunday evening and Vlad had crept
down to the basement to have a chat with
Mulch before his parents woke up. The kind
butler liked to give Vlad treats to make up
for how strict Mortemia and Drax were.

"Thanks for the hot chocolate, Mulch,"
said Vlad. "And the pancakes!" He got up
from the table to take his mug and plate over
to the sink.

"You're welcome, Master Impaler," said
Mulch. He patted Vlad on the shoulder with

his huge hand.

Vlad staggered backwards and lost his balance. "Oh!" he cried.

His mug and plate went flying from his hands, landing with a SMASH! on the hard stone floor.

"Sorry," said the lumbering butler, stooping to clear the mess. "Don't know my own strength sometimes."

Vlad looked sad. "I wish I were as strong as you," he said.

"You will be one day," said Mulch, smiling. "All vampires have super-strength."

"Except me," said Vlad. "Mother is always going on about how I need to get stronger." He pulled a face. "I thought that if I got my Bat Licence she would be proud of me at last. Apparently not – I'm still a rubbish vampire."

"You're not!" Mulch boomed. "Count Drax is proud of you – and Master Gory."

Vlad shrugged. "I s'pose," he said. "But Mother will never be happy with me."

A look of concern flickered across Mulch's craggy features. "Would you like another hot chocolate, Master Impaler?" he asked.

"No, thank you," said Vlad. "I'd better go back to my room. I wouldn't want Mother to catch me down here. We'd both be in trouble then."

Mulch put his head on one side. "You know," he said slowly, "your parents are not as bad as you think they are."

Vlad looked shocked. "Don't let them catch you saying that!" he said. "They're proud of being bad."

Mulch chuckled. "What I mean is, they're not your *enemies*, Master Impaler."

Vlad gave a hollow laugh. "You could've fooled me," he said. "Mother is still threatening to send me to the Black Tower. She's always saying I am a 'disgrace to the vampire race'. And I think that Father secretly wishes that Lupus was his son instead of me."

Lupus was Vlad's cousin. He lived in Transylvania and had come to stay with Vlad. He was brilliant at all the vampire skills. Vlad's father had been very impressed with him, although his mother had actually

found Lupus rather cheeky.

Mulch was shaking his head. "That's not true. They were thrilled with how much you improved your skills while your cousin was here."

"I only managed cos Lupus helped me," Vlad muttered.

"Lupus might have given you some lessons," said Mulch. "But you were the one that passed that test. You did it on your own. I don't think any of us will forget how you swerved to avoid Countess Mortemia!"

Vlad smiled as he remembered. "No, I don't think *she* will either," he said. "She wouldn't have crashed into the yew tree if I hadn't whizzed out of her way like that."

"And then YOU would've crashed instead – and you wouldn't have got your licence," Mulch insisted. "You have excellent bat-manoeuvre skills, Master. You'll learn how

to use the power of super-strength quickly enough as well. Just like you've learned to use mind control. You've come a long way since the tiny scared vampire you once were. In fact," said Mulch, his eyes widening as an idea occurred to him, "do you know what I think?"

Vlad shook his head. "I can't *read* people's minds, Mulch," he said. "Don't tell me that's another vampire skill I'm going to have to learn!"

Mulch gave a booming laugh. "No! Hell's bells, I should think not. Imagine the chaos it would cause if we could read each other's thoughts!"

"Yes," said Vlad, with a shudder. "Mother and Father would be able to listen in on me thinking about school and Minxie…"

"That's just it, though," said Mulch. He was looking excited. "I don't think you should keep that a secret any longer."

Vlad shot up from his chair. "WHAT?" he cried.

Mulch put a hand on Vlad's arm, pinning him to the spot. "Listen," he said. "I think that you've proved yourself to be such a wicked vampire now that you could tell your parents about your visits to human school. I even think you could introduce them to Minxie."

Vlad's pale face turned a shade of green. "NO! They would – they would…" he stammered.

Mulch cracked a huge grin. "They would be amazed," he said.

Vlad was so horrified that he couldn't think what to say to the butler. The words *Mulch has gone mad!* were going round and round inside his head.

"They would be shocked at first, yes," Mulch was saying. "But once they'd got used to the idea, they'd be amazed *and* proud that their son was brave enough to go out in the daytime and go to human school. Your cousin Lupus said he thought you were brave to do that, didn't he? And I think he's right. Not only are you brave, you're also a very good friend – to Lupus, Minxie – even me," he finished. He looked at Vlad sheepishly.

Vlad was astonished. "Do you *really* think that?" he asked.

Mulch nodded.

Vlad groaned. "Mulch, it's all very well you saying such lovely things. But I can't tell Mother and Father. They would lock me up in the Black Tower forever!"

"It's going to get harder and harder to keep it a secret," Mulch said.

Vlad felt himself getting flustered.

"Don't I know it—!" he began, but he was interrupted by an excitable squeaking and fluttering of wings.

Flit, Vlad's pet bat, had flown into the kitchen.

"Quick, Vlad!" Flit shrieked. "Time to get back to your room. I can hear your mother calling you to breakfast!" Flit had super-strong bat hearing, so he could hear things from miles away.

Vlad scrambled down from his chair. "I was just leaving," he said.

Mulch called after the little vampire. "I could be there when you tell them if it would help!"

Vlad ran out of the kitchen without answering.

"What was all that about?" Flit squeaked.

"Don't ask," Vlad replied. "I think Mulch has been eating too much human food and it's upset his brain. He's talking nonsense."

Vlad raced up the stairs from the basement with Flit flying alongside him. Suddenly he brushed Vlad's ear with his wing and whispered, "Stop!"

"What?" Vlad turned to face Flit.

"Mortemia's getting closer to your room," Flit whispered. "I don't think you've got time to—"

"Aha! You're up early," said a voice.

Vlad whipped round and looked up to

see a figure looming over him at the top of the stairs.

"Grandpa!" he breathed. "You gave me a fright."

"Mortemia will be a lot more frightening than me if she catches you down here with Mulch," said Grandpa Gory. "You'd better hurry to the dining room and I'll make an excuse for you."

Vlad skipped up the last few steps and joined Grandpa just as Mortemia appeared in the hallway.

"There you are!" she cried. She was glaring at her son with blood-red eyes. "Why weren't you in your room?"

Grandpa took a step forwards. "I was asking Vlad to show me his latest bat manoeuvres," he said. "He's been practising flying upside down – and getting rather good at it, too."

Vlad swallowed. That was not a helpful thing for Grandpa to have said! Vlad didn't need his mother to be reminded of how he had made her crash.

Sure enough, the mention of flying seemed to make Mortemia more grumpy than ever.

"Harrumph," she said, crossing her arms. "We all know Vlad can fly – at last," she added, with a sneer. "He's still got a long way to go before he could be called a *proper* vampire, though, whatever his father might say." She turned to her son. "What about your super-strength, Vlad?" she asked.

Vlad said nothing.

"Well?" his mother insisted.

Vlad hung his head. "I don't know," he muttered.

Mortemia let out an exasperated noise. "So much for your cousin Lupus teaching you," she said. "I knew that cheeky young devil was a waste of time. We'd better get on with your lessons immediately after breakfast. Unless you want to start Monday morning in the Black Tower?" she added.

"No, Mother," said Vlad quietly.

That just proves it, Vlad thought as he trudged into the dining room behind his mother. *Mulch has no idea what he's talking about – there is no way in a MILLION YEARS that I can tell her I go to human school!*

After breakfast, Vlad followed his parents into the parlour.

"Drax, demonstrate your super-strength please," Mortemia said. "And Vlad, pay attention," she added, shooting him a withering look. "Let's hope you can pick up this skill faster than you learned all the other ones."

No chance, Vlad thought. But out loud he said, "Yes, Mother."

Drax was hesitating, however.

"Well?" Mortemia said to her husband. "What are you waiting for?"

Drax looked doubtful. "I was just wondering why we're bothering with this skill," he said. "It's rather old-fashioned. I mean, does Vlad *really* need super-strength? His mind control is very good now. He could move things with his mind if he needed to—"

"I know all about that, thank you!" Mortemia snapped. "I still haven't forgotten how he shrank me to the size of a spider."

"Yes, that was rather amusing!" said Drax. He caught Vlad's eye and chuckled. Then seeing that his wife did not agree, Drax flashed his sparkling white fangs and said, "What would you like me to lift with my super-strength, my little blood cell?"

Mortemia clicked her tongue. "Something heavy of course! Vlad will watch and then he will attempt to lift the same item."

Please don't choose anything too big, Vlad prayed silently.

He watched as his father looked around the parlour, umming and aahing over what to pick. "How about the bookcase?" Drax said.

Vlad sighed.

"I really don't care, Drax," Mortemia barked. "Just get on with it."

Drax nodded. He stared hard at the bookcase. A strange glow seemed to come from his bloodshot eyes.

Then the Count stepped forward and grasped hold of the bookcase. In seconds he had lifted it up as though it were as light as his breakfast glass of blood.

Vlad gasped. He watched his father carry the heavy piece of furniture over to the other side of the room and set it down next to the grandfather clock.

"Da-daaah!" Drax cried, giving a sweeping bow.

Mortemia rolled her eyes. "No need for that," she said. "We are not about to applaud you."

Drax's face fell. "Shame," he said. "I've always fancied a life on the stage." He winked at Vlad.

Vlad felt his stomach flip. Why had his father said that? He couldn't know that Vlad had auditioned with Minxie for a part in the school show, could he?

But if Drax had meant anything by his comment, he didn't have a chance to say any more. Mortemia was getting impatient.

"Stop fooling around, Drax," she snapped.

"Now, Vlad. I want you to copy your father."

Vlad shook his head. "I can't," he said. "You know I can't."

"You've never tried," his mother retorted. "And besides, for a vampire there is no such word as 'can't'."

Vlad frowned. *Of course there is*, he thought. *I've just said it*. But he knew better than to argue with his mother.

"Come on!" said Mortemia. "We're waiting. And you'd better not try mind control. That would be cheating."

I probably couldn't get mind control to work anyway, Vlad thought. He became so nervous when his mother shouted at him. How on earth had his father found the strength to lift such a heavy object?

Just then he remembered what his cousin Lupus had said to him: *It's all a question of confidence.*

He thought about being on stage in front of his friends at school. He pretended that he was acting out the part of Drax in a school play. Minxie was by his side. It would be fine. All he had to do was imagine that the bookcase was as light as a bat's wing.

Vlad drew back his shoulders and stood up tall, just as his father had done. Then he took a step forward.

But at that exact same moment, he caught sight of his mother glaring at him and he immediately began worrying. What if Mulch knew about the play from hearing Vlad chatting to Lupus and Minxie? What if he had told Drax? What if Drax decided to tell Mortemia?

Vlad shook his head. *I can do this*, he told himself. *I can do this, I can do this.*

He took hold of the bookcase, closed his eyes and heaved with all his might.

Nothing happened.

He tried again.

Nothing.

He pulled and pulled and heaved and strained.

"Oh, for badness' sake!" screeched Mortemia.

Vlad jumped back and landed on his father's toes.

"Argh!" Drax shouted, grabbing hold of his foot and leaping about on one leg. "You clumsy devil!"

"I'm sorry, Father," Vlad said. "Are you all right?"

"Yes," Drax answered, through gritted fangs. "Just hurry up and then we can all get on with our Sunday night in peace and quiet."

"I – I don't think I can lift anything heavy," said Vlad. "Maybe I'm not old enough yet."

Mortemia gave a loud sniff. "Your father could lift a horse and carriage in one hand when he was your age."

What's the use in that? No one even has *a horse and carriage any more,* Vlad thought grumpily.

"All right," he said aloud. He tried to sound reasonable, like Drax when he wanted to persuade Mortemia. "Maybe I just need to start with something smaller? Could I try and lift that table in the corner?"

"No," said Mortemia. "What's the point in moving a table using super-strength? Even a

human could lift that," she scoffed. "It's no good, Vlad. If you can't demonstrate your super-strength skills by the end of the week you will be going to the Black Tower. Some time alone will give you the chance to think about how you are going to work on your skills. I am running out of patience trying to teach you."

Even Drax looked horrified at this. "My little devil," he said to his wife. "No need to be so harsh!"

"Oh, really?" cried Mortemia. "Well, I'm not interested in your opinions, Drax. It was *your* idea to have your nephew Lupus to stay. You SAID that he would teach our son how to be a truly bad vampire. All that has happened is that Vlad now knows how modern-thinking your ridiculous sister and her family are – and he STILL can't show me all the vampire skills!"

"Now, Mortemia, that's not fair—" Drax began.

"ENOUGH!" shrieked Vlad's mother. Then turning to Vlad she said, "Go and practise. You will show me your super-strength by next weekend, or it's the Black Tower for you."

Vlad looked pleadingly at his father but Drax would not meet his eye. "Do as your mother says," he muttered. "Go away and practise."

Vlad escaped to his room. He spent a couple of hours trying to lift his coffin and then his wardrobe and then his oak chest. When he failed at each attempt, he tried using mind control to move them. But even without Mortemia there to put him off, he wasn't very successful. He could make the furniture move a little but he couldn't get it to lift off the ground. A wave of exhaustion swept over him and his brain felt cloudy and dull.

"It's no good!" he complained. "Even if I could use mind control, Mother would know

I've cheated." He collapsed on to his coffin, feeling defeated.

Flit came fluttering down from the ceiling. "You'll get there in the end, Vlad," he said encouragingly. "You always do."

"Not this time," said Vlad. "And I think I know why – I don't really *care* any more. No matter what I do, I won't ever make Mother proud of me. Every time I master a new vampire skill I think I'm going to make her happy but all that happens is she thinks of *another* skill for me to learn – and it's always harder than the last one."

Flit stroked Vlad's head with the tip of his wing. "You know what I think the trouble is?" he said.

"What?" said Vlad.

"I think Mortemia is one of those vampires who will never be happy about anything – it's not just you. She doesn't like living here because there are no other vampires around and she doesn't want to go back to Transylvania because she thinks the vampires there have lost touch with the old way of life. I think she feels as though she doesn't fit in anywhere and that makes her sad and angry."

"It doesn't mean she has to take it out on me!" said Vlad.

"No," Flit agreed, looking thoughtful. "You know, maybe what Mulch said is right," he said. "If you told your family about your human friends, they might *have* to accept that is the way things are now. Perhaps if you got Lupus's parents to write to yours and explain—"

"No way!" Vlad interrupted. "What good would that do? You've just said yourself that Mother doesn't like the way they live."

"All right," Flit said in a soothing tone. "Why don't you read me a story instead? What's that book you brought home from school on Friday?" He pointed to a library book sticking out from under Vlad's coffin.

"*Hansel and Gretel*," Vlad replied. "It's the story that we're making into a play for the school show. Not that I will be in it if I end up in the Black Tower," he added.

"Don't think about that now. Just read to me," said Flit.

"OK," Vlad agreed. He didn't need much persuasion – reading stories always made him feel better.

Vlad opened the book and started reading aloud. As he read about the brother and sister going into the woods and finding the gingerbread house, he began to forget about his mother and her demanding vampire lessons. Instead, in his mind, he became

Hansel, pushing through the undergrowth and coming out into the clearing where the cosy cottage stood. He could almost taste the sweets on the walls as Hansel and Gretel picked them off and ate them.

He finished the story and closed the book, then lay back on his coffin.

"That's a great fairy tale!" Flit squeaked, flying around in happy circles. "I hope you and Minxie get to be Hansel and Gretel. Do you think I could fly into school and hide somewhere so that I could watch the show?"

Vlad said nothing. He was still staring up at the cobwebby ceiling.

Flit fluttered down beside Vlad and stroked his head with his wing. "Look on the bright side, Vlad," he added, glancing at the window. "In a few hours' time it will be daylight and you can escape to school. Then you'll find out what part you've got in the show!"

Vlad nodded. He was distracted, though. All he could think of was Mortemia telling him he would go to the Black Tower if he couldn't master his super-strength.

It won't matter which part I get in the show if I end up being locked away forever, he thought.

Flit hovered above Vlad, looking concerned. "I think you should get some sleep," he said. "No one will come and bother you now. You need to be rested for school."

"I suppose you're right," said Vlad, snuggling down into his coffin. "Goodnight, Flit."

"Goodnight!" Flit squeaked. "I'll wake you in the morning." And he flew up to the rafters and put his head under his wing.

Vlad couldn't sleep, however. He lay staring at Flit, turning anxious thoughts over and over in his mind.

If I don't get a part, Minxie will be upset...

If I DO get a part, I will have to make sure I stay out of the Black Tower...

If my parents find out that I'm in the show, I'll be put in the Black Tower anyway...

Maybe Mulch is right – maybe I should tell my parents the truth about school?

Either way it looks as though I'm going to end up in the Black Tower, so I really don't have anything to lose...

But this last thought was too awful for poor Vlad. He couldn't think of anything worse than being locked away and never seeing Minxie and his other friends again.

He tossed and turned until the night sky began to lighten. Eventually he dropped off to sleep just as dawn crept over the hill and into the graveyard of Misery Manor.

4

The next morning, Vlad crept out of Misery Manor and transformed into a bat so that he could fly to school as usual. He didn't feel as excited as he normally did, though. His wings were heavy and his head was fuzzy with sadness and worry. Even though the sun was shining, Vlad thought he might as well have been flying through a black cloud.

He flew to the bike shed and transformed back into himself just as Minxie arrived. She had borrowed his skateboard over the weekend and had used it to get to school

that morning instead of taking the bus as she usually did. The breeze had ruffled her hair and her cheeks were flushed. She beamed when she saw her friend.

"Hey, Vlad!" she cried. "Thanks for letting me use your skateboard." She shoved it in between two bikes and then threw her arms around Vlad, squashing him into an enormous bear hug. "Today's the day!" she squealed. "They're going to tell us at lunchtime what parts we've got. Are you excited?"

"Hmm," said Vlad.

Minxie pulled away. She examined Vlad's face. "What's up? You look grumpy. Aren't you looking forward to finding out?"

Vlad shrugged. "Maybe," he said.

Minxie put her hands on her hips and fixed Vlad with a stern look. "What happened this weekend?"

"It's Mother…" Vlad began.

"It always is!" said Minxie. She linked her arm through his. "Tell me all about it while we walk to class."

Vlad felt a wave of happiness. No matter how upset he was about things at Misery Manor, Minxie always made him feel better.

The two children made their way across the playground and Vlad told Minxie everything – about the latest vampire skill he had to learn and about his mother threatening to send him to the Black Tower.

He kept his voice low so that no one else could hear.

Minxie listened carefully. Then, when Vlad had finished, she let out a long whistle and said, "Boy oh boy. Your mother is unbelievable! Who on earth needs super-strength these days? We have machines to do that kind of thing."

"What do you mean?" Vlad asked.

"If people are building a house or whatever, then they use cranes and diggers and things. No one actually has to *pick up* huge stones and stuff with their hands!" Minxie exclaimed, waving her arms in the air. "I reckon Lupus was right – your parents are old-fashioned – and MEAN, too. No one locks their kids up in towers." She paused as if thinking hard. Then, her eyes brightening, she said, "Hey! I've got an idea."

Vlad was always nervous when Minxie had

one of her ideas. "What?" he asked.

"Why don't you come and live with me?" she said, beaming.

Vlad felt a rush of warmth. "That is a lovely thing to say, but I can't just run away."

Minxie's face fell. "Why not?"

"Because Mother and Father would come looking for me," Vlad replied.

"Would they?" said Minxie, arching one eyebrow.

Vlad hesitated. Maybe she was right. Maybe they wouldn't. If they were happy to lock him up in the Black Tower, maybe they wouldn't care if he didn't come home at the end of the day.

He felt suddenly very sad. He realized that he didn't belong anywhere – not at home in Misery Manor and not in the human world either. It was all right when he was at school with Minxie. But he

couldn't be with her all the time. Then he remembered what Flit had said about his mother. Would he end up as miserable and angry as her? Would he feel like this for the rest of his life? Vampires lived such a long time. Perhaps he'd feel lonely for hundreds of years…

He was brought back down to earth by Minxie poking his arm. "Hey! I was talking to you!"

"Sorry," said Vlad. "What did you say?"

"I asked if you'd told Mulch what your mum said?" she asked. "He could help, couldn't he?"

"I'm not sure he could," said Vlad. "I think he's gone a bit crazy, actually. He told me I should tell Mother and Father the truth about coming to human school. He says they're not as bad as I think they are – which is ridiculous!"

Vlad expected Minxie to agree with him but instead she looked thoughtful and said, "Perhaps Mulch is right – if you showed your parents how brilliantly you are doing at school, they might stop worrying about you being the perfect vampire."

Vlad opened his mouth to protest but was interrupted by the bell ringing. He silently followed Minxie to join their class for registration.

Vlad spent all morning thinking about what Minxie had said. He couldn't focus on anything else. Minxie wasn't exactly helping with his concentration. The closer it got to lunchtime, the more fidgety she became. She could not sit still. She kept shoving secret notes into Vlad's lap about how excited she was and was told off three times

for "giggling and jiggling". In fact, she was not the only one. Everyone was excited to find out who had got the main parts in the show so there was a lot of chattering and whispering going on.

Miss Lemondrop, meanwhile, was trying to get the class to concentrate on their lesson. "You must settle down," she told the children. "We need to finish our work. Mr Bendigo will be coming in soon to tell you which parts you have in the show. And Malika, can you please stop trying to pass notes to Vlad without me seeing?" she added, with a knowing look at Minxie.

Minxie put on her most innocent expression. "What notes?" she asked, batting her eyelashes.

Miss Lemondrop tutted and shook her head but Vlad noticed that she couldn't help smiling, too. "Your acting skills are good but even I can see what you're up to, Malika."

Minxie got up and did a bow to the class, which made everyone giggle.

The teacher was about to tell her to sit down when there was a loud knock at the door and Mr Bendigo came in, booming, "Hello, Badger Class!"

A babble of excited chatter started up.

"All right, settle down," said Miss Lemondrop. "If you're not quiet you won't hear what parts you've got. One … two … three!" she called and the class was silent.

"OK," said Mr Bendigo importantly. He paused and looked around at the grinning children. "This…" he said, putting on a dramatic voice, "is the moment you've all been waiting for."

Everyone shifted in their seats.

"Are we ready?" Mr Bendigo asked.

"Yes," the class chorused.

"Are you sure?" asked Mr Bendigo. He beamed at Miss Lemondrop.

"YES!" everyone cried impatiently.

Minxie leaned across to nudge Vlad, then she pulled a pretend-scared face and held up both hands, crossing her fingers.

Vlad swallowed. He faced the front and

watched as Mr Bendigo made a big deal out of clearing his throat and shaking out a piece of paper

"Leisha," said Mr Bendigo. "You are…"

Leisha gave a small squeak and jiggled up and down in her seat.

"The witch!" Mr Bendigo announced.

"Eeeeeek!" Leisha squealed in delight as her friends cheered.

"Well done, Leesh!" said Ravi, giving her a high five.

The applause died down. "And you, Ravi…" said Mr Bendigo, "…are…"

Ravi looked worried. "What?" he whispered hoarsely.

"…the woodcutter!" said Mr Bendigo.

"YAY!" Ravi leaped from his seat and began demonstrating his woodcutting by pretending to cut down his chair.

The class laughed.

Miss Lemondrop and Mr Bendigo exchanged amused glances.

"Chitra," Mr Bendigo went on. "You are – the stepmother!"

"Oh yeah!" said Chitra, grinning.

Minxie nudged Vlad and giggled as Mr Bendigo ran through the list of who had got which parts.

Vlad crossed his fingers and sat on his hands. Why was the teacher taking so long? Couldn't he just get to the two main parts and do all the others after?

Minxie was practically jumping up and down in her seat and kept letting out tiny squealing noises. Vlad glanced at her and she beamed widely. Vlad closed his eyes and held his breath. He had never felt so nervous and excited in his life – not even on his first ever day at school. He couldn't bear it! He was going to burst…

Then he heard a loud shriek and felt someone tap him on the shoulder.

"Vlad! Vlad?" It was Mr Bendigo. "Are you all right? You look a bit white – I know it's exciting news but please don't faint on me!"

Vlad looked up at the teacher with a puzzled expression, then he looked across and saw that Minxie had left her desk and was punching the air. "We did it, Vlad!" she shouted. "We're going to be Hansel and Gretel."

Vlad gasped. He leaped up from his desk and punched the air as well. "We really did it!" he cried. Minxie threw her arms round him and the class cheered.

"Well done, both of you," said Miss Lemondrop with a wide smile. "I'm sure your parents will be very proud. And it will be lovely to get the chance to meet yours at last, Vlad."

Vlad felt all the blood drain from his face.

Use mind control! he told himself. *Quick! Stop her from asking any more about Mother and Father!*

Luckily Miss Lemondrop was immediately distracted by Boz.

"It's not FAIR!" he was shouting. He had jumped up and his face was bright red. "How come HE gets the main part? It should be me.

I ALWAYS get the main part!"

"Boswell, go and stand by the door," said Miss Lemondrop. "You know why you didn't get the part this time. You've been in far too much trouble this term…" As she continued to tell Boz off, Boz caught Vlad's eye and glared at him with an expression that made Vlad's heart plummet into his shoes.

"I don't want to stand by the door!" Boz shouted at the teacher.

"You'll do as you're told, Boswell," Miss Lemondrop replied. "Think of it as good practice for your part in the school play – as one of the trees," she added.

Boz howled in frustration and went to stand by the door as he'd been asked.

Minxie sniggered. "I've never seen an angry tree before," she whispered to Vlad.

"That's enough, Malika," said the teacher, but Vlad was sure he saw her lips twitch in a smile as she said this.

Vlad frowned.

"Smile – it's funny!" said Minxie, nudging him.

But Vlad wasn't sure he agreed. Boz had never liked Vlad and was jealous of how popular he had become. He had tried his best to muck up Vlad's audition but thankfully

Vlad's cousin Lupus had saved the day.

He's not going to make life easy for me now that I am the main part, Vlad thought anxiously. *As if I didn't have enough to worry about...*

Minxie caught the expression on Vlad's face.

"Cheer up! Who cares about silly old Boz?" she said, linking her arm through Vlad's.

"You're right," Vlad said, smiling gratefully. "It's going to be great. And it's all thanks to you, too – if you hadn't encouraged me, I would never have been chosen as Hansel."

Minxie gave him a squeeze. "Rubbish," she said. "You're a brilliant actor – we both are! We're the dream team – we're going to be the stars of the show and NO ONE is going to get in our way!"

5

"I can't WAIT for rehearsals, can you?"
Minxie said, as she and Vlad followed their
class out to the playground after lunch.
"D'you think we can choose our own
costumes? I've got this amazing dress with
frills and lace and…"

"Minxie," Vlad cut in. "I – I need to talk
to you."

Minxie stopped in her tracks and put
her hands on her hips. "What?" she asked
suspiciously. "You're not getting nervous,
are you?"

"No," said Vlad. Then he dropped his gaze to his feet. "Kind of," he muttered.

Minxie put her hands on his shoulders. He looked up and saw she had fixed him with one of her determined looks. "You. Are. Brilliant. OK?" she said.

Vlad gave a sheepish grin. "Thanks," he said. "It's not really about the acting, though," he said. He took a deep breath.

"Come and sit down and tell me," said Minxie, and she led him to a bench where they could talk quietly, away from their friends.

"This is about your parents, isn't it?" Minxie said.

Vlad nodded. "I'm worried that I'm going to end up in the Black Tower. If I do, it won't matter how good I am at acting – I won't be able to be in the show!"

Minxie threw up her hands. "You know

what?" she said. "Someone should do something about your parents. It's against the actual law to be nasty to your children. I bet if you told Miss Lemondrop what they're really like – especially about how they say they'll lock you up in the Black Tower and stuff – she'd be able to help you move out. There are people in the government who can help teachers do that," she added importantly.

Vlad thought that Minxie was very probably making up that last bit. In any case, he really didn't want Miss Lemondrop to get involved with his family in any way whatsoever.

"No," he said firmly. "I don't think the human government would be any good at handling vampires – I mean, *you-know-whats*," he added hastily, checking that none of their friends were listening in on their conversation.

"Don't worry about that lot," said Minxie, following Vlad's gaze. "They're not listening. They're too excited about the show."

"Well, anyway," Vlad went on. "I keep telling you: you-know-whats and humans are not supposed to mix."

Minxie put her hands on her hips and looked very doubtful. "But that's not true, is it?" she said. "What about you and me? You're a vamp—"

"Shhh!" Vlad said, putting his finger to his lips.

"All right, all right!" Minxie said. "You're a *you-know-what*," she said, "and I'm a human and – guess what? Nothing terrible has happened."

Vlad opened his mouth to say that he wasn't the same as other vampires.

But Minxie was not going to be put off. "Remember what Lupus said about his school in Transylvania?"

"That's different," Vlad insisted. "*Everything* is different in Transylvania. Lupus is definitely different – he's an excellent you-know-what AND he knows how to fit in with humans. Not like me," he added. "I don't fit in anywhere."

Minxie rolled her eyes. "*Of course* you fit in – you fit in here at school. And you definitely fit in at home – Mulch and Grandpa think so, don't they? Look at all the skills you've learned since we became friends," she said.

"I bet there's loads of other things that you'll end up being able to do as you get older," she added encouragingly.

Minxie is right, Vlad thought. He was a much better vampire than he had been when he first met Minxie. "Why do you think Mother and Father are so disappointed in me, then?" he asked.

Minxie pulled a face and shrugged. "Parents are weird," she said. "I suppose they're just trying to teach you stuff. I mean, if there was a school for vamp— *you-know-whats*, you'd be learning those things just like we humans have to learn our times tables and our spellings," she pointed out. "We aren't born knowing how to do all that human stuff, so why should you be born knowing all *your* skills? You just have to stand up to your mother and tell her that. She's probably too old to remember what

it was like being our age."

Minxie had a point. Vlad's parents were ancient. It was over a hundred years since they had been his age.

Minxie was looking at Vlad carefully. "I still think you should talk to Miss Lemondrop, though. She's very kind. *She* knows you're not scary or frightening. I bet she wouldn't even care if you told her what you and your family really are."

But this was too much for Vlad. "No!" he whispered. "I get what you're saying about the skills and maybe I should try talking to Mother. But there's no way I can EVER let anyone else at school know that I am a you-know-what," he said. "And *you* promised you would keep it a secret," he added. "No, I'll just have to keep doing what I have been doing up until now – keeping school a secret from home and home a secret from school."

But even as he said it he wasn't sure how much longer he could do that.

When the bell rang, they ran to line up to go back into class. But Miss Lemondrop had an announcement.

"There's been a change of plan this afternoon," said the teacher. "I want you all to go straight to the hall. You are to put on your costumes and line up on the stage."

"No way am I dressing up as a stupid tree – not now, not NEVER," Boz muttered. He leaned forward and poked Vlad. "YOU should be a tree," he said. "Because it doesn't matter what you look like. Your family won't even be coming to the show, will they Mr Freaky-Teeth? Unless you count that huge ugly monster who lives in your house!"

Vlad froze. He hoped no one had heard

that! Boz had followed him home one night and met Mulch. The butler had picked Boz up and thrown him out of the house! That was yet *another* reason why Boz didn't like Vlad.

"Boswell, stop talking and listen," said Miss Lemondrop sternly.

Vlad breathed a sigh of relief as he realized she hadn't heard what Boz had said. She had already turned her attention to the rest of the class.

"Mrs Viola has said she would like a special photograph of Badger Class. A professional photographer is coming to take the picture. Mrs Viola is going to send it to the local paper—"

Everyone began chattering at this exciting news.

Everyone except Vlad. He felt panic rise in his chest as Miss Lemondrop went on speaking.

A photo! he thought. *No! I can't be in a photo!*

Minxie saw Vlad's expression and said, "You mustn't let Boz upset you."

"It's not that," said Vlad, as the children pushed and jostled their way to the hall. "It's the photo…"

Minxie was looking at him strangely. "What's the problem? I mean, I know some people don't like having their photo taken but it's not THAT bad."

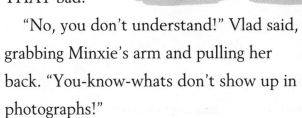

"No, you don't understand!" Vlad said, grabbing Minxie's arm and pulling her back. "You-know-whats don't show up in photographs!"

Minxie looked puzzled. "Sorry?"

"Grandpa told me once," Vlad whispered. "There are no photos of you-know-whats anywhere. We can't see ourselves in mirrors either."

Minxie gasped. "That's amazing!" she said.

"When I asked Mother about it she said it was 'a good thing'," said Vlad, putting on his "Mortemia voice". "She said, 'Mirrors make humans vain which is why they are so stupid.'"

Minxie laughed as she always did when Vlad did impressions of his family.

But Vlad didn't join in. Thinking of his mother made him feel sicker than ever.

Everything about this show is turning into a nightmare! he thought. *Why did I let Minxie talk me into auditioning? How am I going to get out of this?*

The answer was: he couldn't. There was no way Vlad could escape.

6

Once the children were dressed and ready, they were herded on to the stage.

"Stand still, please!" Mrs Viola called out. "I want a nice neat group for the photo."

As the Head Teacher organized everyone into one long line, a photographer arrived and began setting up her camera on a tripod.

"Vlad and Minxie, I want you to be at the front, in the centre of the photo, please," said Mrs Viola. "As you are the stars!" she added, with a sparkly smile.

"Stars – huh," Boz muttered, squeezing

in behind Vlad. "Move!" he growled, giving Vlad a shove. "And take that stupid hat off," he said, grabbing the little cap that Vlad had been given as part of his costume. "No one will be able to see *my* face."

Minxie turned around and said, "That would be a good thing, Boz." Then she stuck her tongue out.

"Hey!" Boz glared.

"I don't think I want to be in the photo anyway," Vlad began.

"Yeah, good idea – why don't you go home?" Boz said. "Oh, sorry, you don't have a home, do you? Unless you count that spooky old place at the top of the hill—"

"Stop being mean!" Minxie said in a loud voice.

"What's going on?" Miss Lemondrop called out.

"Watch it, Minxie," Boz said. "You and

your boyfriend are getting on my nerves."

"For the six hundred and fiftieth time: he's NOT my boyfriend," Minxie said through gritted teeth.

Boz reached out and pulled Minxie's hair.

"Boswell Jones!" shouted Miss Lemondrop. "Stop that – move to the end of the line."

"It wasn't me – it was Vlad!" Boz protested.

"Boswell," said Mrs Viola in a warning tone. "Move."

Boz huffed and puffed and pushed through the other children to get to the end of the line. Vlad knew he should feel relieved that he'd gone but he was now more worried than ever that the focus was on him and Minxie. He pulled the cap down over his face as far as it would go.

Maybe if the cap covers my face my body might show up in the photo, he thought.

"Quiet, please!" the photographer called. A hush fell on the crowd. "I'm going to have to take three or four photos," she explained. "So please stand *very* still."

"Why so many?" Vlad whispered to Minxie.

"They always do this for school photos," Minxie said importantly. "It's in case someone moves and makes it all blurry."

This made Vlad feel even more nervous. He might have got away with not showing up in only *one* photo – they might think it was a problem with the camera. But if he didn't show up in *all* the photos, what then?

He looked around wildly but it was no good – he was wedged in between Minxie and Ravi.

"Ready?" the photographer called out. "I'll count to three, then you give me your best smile…" She bent down to look through her camera and called out, "One … two … three!" Then she took a photo.

Just after she said, "Three!" there was a small commotion at the end of the line

behind Vlad.

Vlad didn't dare turn to see what it was. He didn't want to draw any attention to himself.

"No moving, please!" cried the photographer, adjusting the camera slightly. "Ready again? One … two … three!"

There was another ripple of noise somewhere behind Vlad. He kept his head down and stood as still as he could.

Maybe if I'm as rubbish a vampire as Mother says I am, I will be in the picture after all, he thought.

"Please," the photographer said, frowning. "You *must* stand still."

"What is going on?" Miss Lemondrop said, stepping forward.

"There's some wriggling about," said the photographer. She stood back to check the rows of children. "That's better. Ready?"

Vlad stared straight ahead as the photographer said her final, "One ... two ... three..."

At last the photographer was finished. She picked her camera up off the tripod and began flicking through the images on the screen.

Vlad's heart was thumping in his chest. Would she see that his face wasn't in the photo?

While the photographer was checking the images, Mrs Viola told everyone to line up to get ready to change back into their uniforms.

"There, that wasn't so bad, was it?" Minxie asked, as they began filing off the stage.

Vlad let go of the breath he'd been holding. "No," he admitted. *It looks as though I've got away with it!* he thought.

But just as he was about to completely relax, the photographer cried, "Oh no!"

She looked up, frowning at the children and then back down at her camera. Then she came over to Mrs Viola and began pointing at the images and gesturing to the stage.

The Head Teacher turned to face the class. She looked extremely cross.

Everyone stopped moving. No one said a word. It was clear something was wrong. Vlad felt so nervous he wasn't sure he could walk without his knees knocking together.

"What's going on?" Minxie asked. "Can we go now, Miss Lemondrop?"

Vlad felt faint. He closed his eyes...

The photographer must have noticed a big hole where he was supposed to be standing...

He had ruined the school photo, just like Boz had warned him not to...

Worse than that, what if everyone knew that vampires didn't show up in photos? What if everyone had figured out what he was? He might actually be in danger!

What should he do? He was too panicky to use mind control. His brain felt as though it were full of noise. He couldn't concentrate. He couldn't breathe. He wished he had magic powers like the fairies in Grandpa's

Encyclopedia of Curious Creatures.

The noise level had begun to rise. Vlad put his hands over his ears and dared not open his eyes in case everyone was about to turn on him.

Maybe I should turn into a bat and fly away and never come back!

"Class, be quiet, *please*," said Mrs Viola, raising her voice. "The pictures haven't come out properly."

Vlad froze. Mrs Viola was going to want to know why he hadn't shown up in the photo!

Suddenly he felt a pinch on his arm. He opened his eyes to see Boz. "Looks as though the camera is broken or something. Your freaky face probably did it," Boz sneered.

Vlad gulped. Did Boz know? Vlad didn't want to wait to find out. He turned to push through the crowd and run, but then

the Head Teacher called out: "BOSWELL JONES!"

"What?" said Boz rudely.

"You can wipe that smirk off your face, young man. You have RUINED the school photograph!" said Mrs Viola.

"No, I haven't," said Boz.

"You certainly have. There is a blurry blob in all the photos where you should have been," said Mrs Viola. "You were moving around after you were specifically told not to."

"I had to, didn't I?" Boz shouted. "There wasn't enough room for my stupid branches."

Mrs Viola's face turned bright pink. "That's it. I've had enough of your bad behaviour this term, Boswell," she said. "Come with me." She beckoned to Boz. "You can do your lessons in my office for the rest of the day."

"No," said Boz. He refused to move. "If

anyone should be going with you, it's Vlad,"
he said.

Everyone muttered in disbelief. No one
had ever dared to speak to the Head Teacher
like that before. Not even Boz.

"He's going to be in BIG trouble now!"
Minxie whispered.

But Vlad had seen the glint in Boz's eye
and he wasn't so sure…

"Boswell—" Mrs Viola began.

"Vlad shouldn't be at this school in the
first place. Isn't it obvious?" said Boz, butting
in. He took a step to the front of the stage.
"None of you have worked it out yet, have
you?" he said. He paused. He was obviously
enjoying himself.

"What are you talking about?" asked Miss
Lemondrop. "Of course Vlad should be
here."

"Oh yeah?" said Boz. "Even though he

lives in a spooky mansion far out of town
on his own with only a giant monster for
company? Even though he can make people
do things with his mind? Even though his
parents have never come to pick him up
from school? Even though he sleeps in …
a COFFIN?"

The class gasped.

"A coffin? Nonsense!" scoffed Mrs Viola.

Minxie grabbed Vlad's arm. "It's OK," she
whispered. "They'll never believe him." She
took a step towards Boz. "I'll shut him up,"
she said over her shoulder.

"I don't think you'll want Vlad to be in the
show – or even this school – when you find
out what he really is," said Boz. He had an
evil grin on his face as he looked around at
his classmates.

Suddenly lots of things happened at once.
Everything happened so fast that Vlad didn't

have time to think about using mind control.

Minxie made a lunge towards Boz to shut him up…

Boz turned at the exact same moment to point at Vlad…

His tree costume caught Ravi in the face and sent him falling back into Minxie…

Minxie screamed, "Vlad – RUN!"

And Boz yelled, "HE'S A VAMPIRE!"

Vlad leaped in fright and, without thinking, shouted aloud, "Bat – Air – Travel!" then…

POOF!

He turned into a bat and whizzed to the door. He took one last look at his friends.

They were all staring at him, speechless with shock. Even Mrs Viola said nothing. Her face was as white as a ghost and her eyes looked as though they would pop out of her head.

Mother and Father were right – everyone's terrified of me! Vlad thought. *I've got to get out of here before they do something awful.*

"It'll be all right, Vlad!" Minxie shouted. "I'll explain!"

But Vlad wasn't going to hang around. He turned and zoomed out of the school hall and into the playground. Tears streamed down his tiny bat face as he realized he would never see Minxie or any of his human friends ever again.

Boz had got what he wanted. He had ruined everything.

Poor Vlad wept as he flew. His worst nightmare had come true.

I'll have to spend the rest of my days at Misery Manor now, learning stupid vampire skills which are no good to anyone. I'll be lonely and miserable forever! he thought.

All he wanted to do was to change back into his vampire form, go to his room and flop into his coffin with the bedcovers pulled over his head. How would he be able to explain to Flit what had happened? The little bat had told him to be careful from the very

first day he set foot in the human school. Would Vlad and his family even be safe at Misery Manor now that the whole school knew? Would Mrs Viola bring those people from the government that Minxie had talked about? Would he and his family be taken away somewhere?

Vlad realized he knew very little about the human world. He felt stupid for not finding out the reasons why humans and vampires didn't mix.

I should have been more careful, he thought. *But how did Boz work it out?*

Vlad landed with a BUMP under the yew tree, back in vampire form. He ran to the front door of Misery Manor.

At least I'm safe for now, he thought. *Boz won't bring anyone here because he's too frightened of Mulch.*

However, as soon as he walked in through

the door of Misery Manor Vlad felt that he was not safe at all. The atmosphere was very wrong. The hall was always cold and draughty, but this afternoon the air in the vast room had an icy chill. And it was darker than normal. It was as though the house itself were hiding from something, frozen with fear.

What is it? Vlad thought.

He wrapped his cape tightly around himself and tiptoed to the bottom of the stairs, using his night-vision to help him in the gloom.

No one from school – or even the government – could have got here that fast – could they?

Vlad winced as he stepped on a loose floorboard and a loud creak echoed off the dark walls.

I shall have to tread very, very carefully so as not to wake Mother and Father, he thought. He took

two more steps. Then:

"SO!"

Vlad gasped, looking up sharply.

Mortemia was standing on the stairs, her hands on her hips. She was glaring down at Vlad, her bloodshot eyes wide, her mouth a tight line of displeasure.

"*This* is what you get up to when you are supposed to be in your coffin?" she said. "No wonder you are half asleep in your lessons!"

Vlad couldn't breathe. His chest was tight. His legs were shaking. He didn't think he would be able to move or speak ever again.

"What have you got to say for yourself?" asked his mother.

Vlad shook his head. "I – I don't know," he whispered.

"Don't bother coming up with some far-fetched story," said his mother. "Your father and I know everything, so there's no point."

Drax appeared next to Mortemia, looking every bit as stern. "Yes, young devil. I think you had better come into my study. I need to have a word with you."

Mortemia scoffed. "There's no need for that," she said. She pulled a piece of parchment from inside her cape and waved it at Vlad. "This letter has told us everything we need to know. It's straight to the Black Tower with you, and no arguments!"

Vlad gasped. "What letter? What are you talking about?"

Drax held out a hand to stop Mortemia from swooping down on Vlad. "He deserves a chance to explain himself," he said.

"He does not!" said Mortemia. "The explanation is all here – as clear as moonlight." She shook the piece of parchment at Vlad. "*This* is a letter from your Aunt Pavlova," she said. "She was writing to

thank us for having
Lupus to stay."

For a moment
Vlad was confused.
What was so bad
about that? But then
his mother went on,
and the words she said
made Vlad feel faint with fear.

"She says that you were very kind
to your cousin and that he had a lovely time
– MEETING ALL YOUR FRIENDS AT
SCHOOL!"

Vlad's head was spinning.

I'm done for! Vlad thought. *I can't run back
to school and I can't stay here! Where will I go?* He
looked around wildly as if a solution would
suddenly appear in the shape of a secret door
or a magic escape route.

Drax coughed. "It seems that you've been

rather taken with the way they do things in Transylvania," he said awkwardly. "Perhaps you think life would be better over there? Would you like to go and live with Lupus? I can easily fix it for you to go and stay with my sister—" Drax began in a kindly tone.

"NO!" cried Mortemia. "What kind of a punishment would that be? Our son clearly LIKES the way your ridiculous sister and her family lives. He obviously thinks that the old vampire ways are not good enough for him."

"It's not that!" Vlad protested. "It's just that I was lonely."

"And you can stay being lonely for a long, long time!" Mortemia screeched. "IN THE BLACK TOWER!" She glared at her son, her eyes glowing red.

Vlad felt himself go limp…

…his head began swimming…

…and his legs collapsed under him…

He woke hours later to find himself lying on a cold stone floor. The room was pitch-black. Vlad lifted his head and groaned. He ached all over. His head was throbbing and his arms and legs were stiff and sore. He sat up slowly and rubbed his eyes. The darkness closed in around him. He couldn't see a thing.

"Wh-where am I?" he said aloud.

"...*AM I?... am I?...* am I?..." his voice echoed back at him.

Then memories of the past few hours came flooding back. He remembered the dreadful scene at school with Boz shouting, "HE'S A VAMPIRE!" He thought of the looks on his friends' faces and Mrs Viola's horrified expression. He remembered turning into a bat and racing home, only to be confronted by his parents.

"I'm in the Black Tower!" Vlad whispered.

He got up shakily and walked forwards with his arms out.

"Oh!" he cried as his hands brushed against damp stone walls.

He walked around, feeling the walls, hoping he might stumble across a coffin to lie on or a candle and some matches so that he could see.

90

He found nothing. Nothing but cold, clammy stone walls and the hard stone floor.

Even if there were some light, it wouldn't be much use, Vlad thought miserably. *I've got no books to read and no parchment to write on. I haven't even got Flit to talk to.*

He leaned against the wall and slid down until he was sitting on the flagstones once more.

What am I going to do? he thought. *I can't get a message to Minxie, and anyway, what would she be able to do? I'm going to be left up here forever!*

He let his face fall into his hands and began to sob again. He sobbed and sobbed until he exhausted himself. Then he curled up into a ball and fell asleep.

He was woken some time later by something tickling his right ear.

"Urgh!" he shrieked, brushing at his ear in a panicked way. "Get off!" He thought it was one of the hundreds of spiders that lived in every room in Misery Manor.

But it wasn't.

"It's me," said a small voice.

"Flit! Is that really you?" Vlad jumped up and whacked the little bat on the nose in his excitement.

"OW!" Flit complained. "What's happened to your night-vision?"

Vlad whirled around in the dark, trying to focus on Flit's voice. "I don't know. It's SO dark in here, it's blacker than night. I'd need some kind of *extra*-super superpower to be able to see."

"Try turning into a bat," said Flit.

"OK," said Vlad.

He concentrated hard. "B – A – T," he whispered.

Nothing happened.

"What's the matter?" asked Flit.

"I – I don't know," Vlad said, his voice trembling. "I – I think it's just – I'm s-s-so frightened!"

"All right, we'll sort this out, don't worry," said Flit, landing on Vlad's shoulder. He nestled comfortingly against the little vampire's ear.

"Oh, Flit," Vlad said. "Thank goodness you've come. But how did you know I was in the Black Tower? How did you get in?"

"I was waiting for you. I knew your parents had got the letter because I heard them talking. It came by Bat Express, which woke them up. I can't *believe* Lupus was stupid enough to tell his parents about your school!"

Vlad was about to agree, but then he remembered all the good things his cousin

had taught him and how he had saved him from Boz during the auditions. "I don't think he meant to get me in trouble," he said. "He must have forgotten that things here aren't like they are in Transylvania – his parents think it's wonderful to have human friends, remember?"

Flit huffed. "Hmm. Well, let's not waste time talking about that now. We need to think about how to get you out. It's easy for me – there are cracks in the brickwork so I can squeeze in and out. If you turned into a bat, you could follow me."

"But I can't!" said Vlad. "I just tried."

"What about your super-strength?" Flit asked. "You might be able to push open the door."

"No. I haven't got super-strength, have I? I've failed at that, too," Vlad said.

Flit gave a sad squeak. Then he had an

idea. "What about if I fly to Minxie and tell her what's happened? She could help."

"NO!" Vlad cried. "She can't help me. Not now everyone knows…" he tailed off in despair.

"Everyone knows what?" Flit asked.

Vlad gave a heavy sigh. "You're going to find out sooner or later, I suppose," he said.

Then he told Flit about how Boz had revealed Vlad's secret.

Flit was so shocked, he leaped up and began fluttering fearfully above Vlad's head.

"So you see," Vlad finished. "I'm stuck here for good."

Flit gave another, even sadder squeak. "That *is* bad," he said. He paused for so long that Vlad thought he'd flown away.

"Flit?" he called out anxiously.

"It's all right, I'm still here," said Flit, landing on Vlad's shoulder again. "I was just thinking… Minxie's your friend, and she's not someone who would give up easily. She'll help you out, I'm sure of it. I think I should go and find her and see if I can get her to follow me here."

"But she doesn't speak bat language!" Vlad cried.

Flit didn't answer. He had already gone.

And Vlad was left alone again in the cold dark tower.

Vlad curled into a ball again to try and keep warm. *I must stay positive*, he told himself. *That's what Minxie would do.*

Flit was right – Minxie was not someone who would give up easily. In fact, Vlad realized, if Minxie were locked up in the Black Tower, she would try a lot harder to turn into a bat so that she could escape. She wouldn't just try once and then sink into despair like Vlad had. And Flit was right about something else, too: Minxie would want to help Vlad.

She wouldn't just forget about me. She might even be on her way here right now without Flit! he told himself.

Thinking of Minxie making her way towards Misery Manor made Vlad more determined than ever to escape.

I can't let her come here on her own, though, he said to himself. *Mother might see her! I need to get out so that I can be here to meet her. Then we'll ... we'll...*

Vlad wasn't sure what they would do next but he decided to worry about that once he had escaped. He couldn't bear to stay in that cold dark tower for a moment longer.

He put all his energy into thinking of transforming into a bat.

He imagined that he was Flit...

He pictured his arms turning into Flit's tiny fluttering wings...

He thought about his ears growing as large as Flit's…

Then he gave a little jump and whispered, "B – A – T!"

And POOF! He was a bat!

Then he was soaring up and around the Black Tower, looking for the cracks in the brickwork that Flit had told him about. Now that he was a bat, his night-vision was much better and soon he had found a gap to squeeze through.

He pushed his head into the small hole, folded his wings behind him, held his breath and wriggled and wriggled until his head peeped out the other side.

"Phew!" he breathed. He gulped in the cool evening air and looked up.

The sky was full of shimmering stars and a full moon hung above Misery Manor, shining brightly to light his way.

"I can do this!" Vlad said aloud. "I can get out of here and find Minxie!"

He gave one final wriggle and then, like a cork coming out of a bottle – POP! – he was free.

It was only then that he realized he had no idea where to go to look for Minxie.

She won't be at school now it's dark, he thought. *And I don't know where she lives!*

"What am I going to do?" he said aloud.

"You're going to come with me!" said a squeaky voice.

Vlad whirled around. "Flit!" he cried.

"No time to chat," said Flit. "Come on." Without waiting for a reply, he whizzed off in the direction of the front door of the manor.

"I can't go back in there!" Vlad cried.

But Flit did not even turn around. "Trust me!" he squeaked.

Vlad swallowed. He had always trusted Flit and the little bat had never let him down. He would have to do as Flit said. It wasn't as if he had any other great plans.

So, taking a deep breath, Vlad zoomed off after Flit.

I just hope he knows what he's doing, he thought.

As Vlad approached the mansion, he saw that the front door was open. Flit flew

straight in. Vlad could hear snatches of conversation drifting up on the breeze. He stopped in mid-air and hovered above the open door, listening carefully.

"…Vlad … doing so well…"

That doesn't sound like Mother, he thought. He moved closer.

"…don't understand…"

He recognized *that* voice!

"…why would you be so MEAN?"

Minxie?

Flit must have found her!

"MINXIE!" Vlad yelled. "YOU'RE HERE!"

But of course even if she had heard him she wouldn't have understood him, because she couldn't speak bat language.

"You can't leave him locked up on his own!" Vlad heard Minxie go on.

"I – I agree with Malika," said another,

slightly shaky, voice.

Miss Lemondrop! Vlad gasped.

"Oh, you do, do you?" said a voice that Vlad recognized only too well.

Mother? NO! Vlad thought.

In that moment, Vlad knew that he couldn't hang back a moment longer. His teacher and his best friend had come right into Misery Manor to find him, with no thought for their own safety, and now here they were, face to face with his mother. He didn't like to think of what Mortemia might do to two humans who had dared to enter her home. And he wasn't going to stop to think about it either.

With a swoop and a dive Vlad whizzed in through the open door of Misery Manor. There, standing with their backs to him were Minxie and Miss Lemondrop and facing them were Drax and Mortemia. Vlad's mother's

face was a picture of fury – her blood-red eyes were flashing and her mouth was pinched tight.

Vlad gritted his fangs. *This is it!* he thought. Then, focusing on the gap between the humans and his mother, he whispered V- L – A – D and flew towards the little group. He landed and transformed back into his vampire form as smoothly as his cousin Lupus would have done.

Mortemia's eyes widened in shock but she quickly recovered.

"So," she said to Vlad, her hands on her hips. "You have added disobedience *and* escape to your long list of mistakes! And, to top it all, it seems that you have some *human* visitors," she added, gesturing to Minxie and Miss Lemondrop.

Drax took a step towards Vlad. "What have you been up to, young devil?" he asked.

Vlad could have sworn that his father's mouth twitched in a smile. He felt very confused. "I – er…" he began.

But he didn't have a chance to say anything, because Minxie had rushed towards Vlad and had grabbed him from behind in the most enormous bear hug.

"Vlad!" she cried. "Poor, poor Vlad – are you all right? How did you survive being locked up in that horrible dark tower?"

"Of course he's all right," snapped Mortemia. "Vampires are used to the dark."

"Yeah well, Vlad doesn't like it," Minxie snapped back, letting go of Vlad.

Vlad's heart jumped into his mouth. "You can't speak to Mother like that!" he said in a hoarse voice.

"Watch me," Minxie whispered. Then she squared up to Mortemia, holding her chin high. "Vlad *hates* the dark," she said to Vlad's mother. "But you already know that, which is why you locked him up, isn't it? You are the meanest person I've ever met. I told you didn't I, Miss Lemondrop?" she said, turning to the teacher. "They just don't get that Vlad wants to go to school and have human friends!"

Mortemia's eyes were bulging out of her head. She opened her mouth to reply but Miss Lemondrop got in first.

"Now, Malika," she said with exaggerated calm. "There is no need to be rude. We are in Mr and Mrs Impalers' house and we must still remember our manners, even if the situation is a little … unusual." Minxie folded her arms and glowered at Mortemia.

"Mrs Impaler," Miss Lemondrop turned to Mortemia, trying to sound reasonable, "could we possibly sit somewhere a little more … comfortable and talk about this?"

"I am COUNTESS Impaler!" shrieked Mortemia. "And we don't have anywhere *comfortable*."

Miss Lemondrop took a hasty step back.

"Countess," said a deep, booming voice. "I have taken the liberty of bringing some refreshments."

It was Mulch! The butler loomed in the hallway behind Mortemia.

Vlad's head was spinning. Everything was

completely out of control! What was Mulch doing? He glanced at Miss Lemondrop who looked as though she might faint from shock at seeing the giant butler. The blood had drained from her face and she opened and shut her mouth like a panicky goldfish.

"Mulch!" cried Minxie. She pushed past Mortemia and ran forward to throw her arms around the butler's enormous knees. "Boy, am I glad to see you."

Mortemia's pale face flushed dark with anger. "How – what – why…?" she stammered. "I will not have this—!" She now seemed more shocked than Vlad's teacher!

"Good heavens," breathed Miss Lemondrop. "What a fascinating home life you have, Vlad!"

Vlad didn't know what to say. Flit seemed to know how he was feeling, and stayed right by him.

Drax meanwhile had taken hold of his wife's arm. "Come, come, my little blood cell," he was saying. "Let's not lose our cool in front of our guests." Then, turning to the butler, he said, "Would you be so kind as to take the refreshments to the parlour please, Mulch?"

Vlad saw that Miss Lemondrop was looking carefully from Mulch to Minxie to Drax, as though she were trying to make

sense of everything. He didn't blame her. How on earth was this going to end? Were the refreshments a trap? Would his parents lock Miss Lemondrop and Minxie up in the Black Tower, too? Would they use mind control on them?

He looked at Minxie. She simply shrugged and said, "Sounds good to me, Count Impaler. I don't know about the rest of you but I'm *starving*."

"I'm sure you are," said Drax, putting on his most charming voice. "Well, what are we are waiting for? Mulch – let's eat."

Mortemia muttered a response that no one heard. Meanwhile Drax ushered everyone out of the hallway and through to the parlour, with Mulch leading the way.

9

Drax chatted to Miss Lemondrop as they walked. "So you're Vlad's teacher," he said. "Tell me, how is the little devil doing in his lessons?"

Miss Lemondrop seemed grateful for some normal conversation. "Vlad is doing very well at school," she replied. "It would be a pleasure to show you his work."

"Wonderful!" Drax replied, flashing a smile.

Why was Drax being so nice to Miss Lemondrop? Vlad glanced at Minxie again, but she just gave him a quick thumbs up.

"Don't worry!" she mouthed.

Vlad looked at Flit and the little bat squeaked, "She's right!"

Meanwhile, it seemed as though Mortemia had given up trying to say or do anything. She kept flashing Drax evil looks, but her husband was ignoring her and giving Miss Lemondrop his full attention instead.

It's as though Mother's lost all her powers! Vlad thought.

The strange group of humans and vampires – and Flit – arrived in the parlour to find Grandpa Gory snoozing in a chair by the fire.

Mulch set down the tray of refreshments. It was as if he served tea to humans at Misery Manor every day of the week.

If Grandpa wakes up and sees Minxie and Miss Lemondrop here it will be a TOTAL disaster, Vlad thought. *What hope will two humans have against THREE grown-up vampires?*

"Will that be all, Master, Mistress?" Mulch asked, looking to Drax and Mortemia in turn.

Mortemia found her voice at last. "YES, THAT WILL BE ALL—!" she roared.

Grandpa Gory interrupted with the most enormous snore. "SNOOOARRGH!"

Vlad jumped. Flit whizzed up to the rafters and Minxie giggled.

Mortemia huffed and Drax rolled his eyes.

Miss Lemondrop looked alarmed.

And Grandpa Gory kept on sleeping!

"This place is turning into a madhouse!" cried Mortemia.

Drax laid a hand on Mortemia's arm. "Now, now," he said. Then, turning to Mulch, he said, "Fetch some blankets for Miss Lemondrop and Malika, please. It's rather chilly in here and I don't think they are as used to the cold as we are."

"Certainly, Master," said Mulch, bowing low.

"Thanks, Mulch!" chirped Minxie, plonking herself down on a sofa.

The butler left the room as everyone took a seat.

Drax poured the tea and handed Miss Lemondrop a cup.

"It's very kind of you to invite us in," she said, taking the drink. "I've often wondered who lived here. It's funny we've never met before."

"Actually, we didn't invite you!" Mortemia muttered. "And it's *not* funny we've never met – that's the way things should be. Vampires and humans are not supposed to mix." She took a loud slurp of tea. "URGH!" she spluttered, putting down her cup and saucer with a clatter. "What's *this*? Where's my glass of blood?"

Drax smiled and patted his wife's knee. "It's tea, dear. It's what all the vampires in

115

Transylvania are drinking these days. Unless you'd prefer hot chocolate?"

Vlad was so confused he didn't know what to think. He glanced from his teacher to his best friend and back again. Why was his father being so polite? Why wasn't anyone scared of Mortemia?

"Can I have a biscuit?" Minxie asked.

"Of course," said Drax, passing her the plate. "Take two!" He took one himself and popped it into his mouth. "Chocolate chip – delicious!" he said through a mouthful of crumbs.

"Biscuit?" said Grandpa Gory, waking with a start. "Did someone say 'biscuit'? Oh, guests, too!" he said, looking around and blinking. "We haven't had guests for at least one hundred years. Are you going to introduce me, Mortemia?"

This was too much for Mortemia. "NO!" she yelled. "Mulch!" she called for the butler. "MULCH! Come back here this instant and get rid of these … these humans!"

"Humans?" cried Grandpa, getting up from his chair. He made his way unsteadily over to Miss Lemondrop, peering at her as though she were a specimen under a

microscope. "My badness me! I never thought I would live to see the day…"

Miss Lemondrop smiled at Grandpa, then to Mortemia she said, "You should be proud of your son, you know."

"PROUD? Of Vlad? Why? He's the worst vampire in the world. He doesn't like blood, he took years to learn how to change into a bat, he's frightened of the dark, spiders, and cobwebs…" She tailed off and looked lost. "I've no idea what is happening to this family. All I've ever done is try and uphold the vampire traditions that are dying out. I blame you, Drax. You and your wretched sister and her family."

"But Vlad is a wonderful vampire!" Miss Lemondrop protested. She frowned, then turned and gestured to Minxie. "Malika has told me about all the special skills he has. And our Head Teacher watched him turn into a bat before her very eyes. *And* he's very proud of his family," she added, smiling. "He's drawn the most beautiful family tree. I brought it to show you. Look." She bent down to place her drink carefully on the floor before reaching for her bag which was at her feet.

Vlad stared, open-mouthed, as his teacher produced from her bag the family tree he had drawn on his first day at human school. What would Mortemia say when she saw that Vlad had told everyone the names of all his vampire relatives?

Vlad held his breath and waited for the explosion he was sure would come.

However, Mortemia did not stamp her feet and shout. Instead she looked at the family tree very carefully. Then something happened which Vlad had never seen before.

A big fat tear rolled down Mortemia's cheek!

Drax looked alarmed and immediately
rushed to his wife's side. "Why are you crying,
my little blood cell? Do you miss the family?
We could go back to Transylvania if you like?

I have been thinking for a while now that it's time we moved out of this creaky old house," he babbled. "We live on this hill, far away from everyone and everything else. We're completely isolated. It's not good for Vlad. He needs friends his own age. I don't think it's good for us either."

"It's not that," sobbed Mortemia. "Look!" she thrust Vlad's family tree at Drax.

Drax looked at it, making approving noises. He passed it to Grandpa Gory.

"Wonderful!" Grandpa declared.

Vlad couldn't believe what he was seeing. Was his family on his side after all?

"He's got all the names here. Every single one. All of our family who are now dead and gone." Mortemia sniffed.

"Not all," said Drax. "We have family in Transylvania."

Mortemia wiped her nose on her sleeve.

"*Your* family," she grumbled. "If it wasn't for your family we would never have had Lupus come to stay – and he wouldn't have put stupid ideas into Vladimir's head about being friends with humans."

"Actually I was friends with Minxie long before Lupus came along," Vlad said quietly.

"Yes," said Minxie. "AND Vlad was a good vampire before Lupus came," she said. "It's just that *you* can never see the things he's good at." She glared at Mortemia. "Anyway, being an excellent friend is much more important than being a perfect vampire, if you ask me." She grinned and squeezed Vlad's hand.

Vlad grinned back. For the first time he allowed himself to believe that everything was going to be all right.

He looked across as his teacher, who was nodding and smiling encouragingly.

"Malika has a point," Miss Lemondrop
said. "It was wonderful to meet Lupus but
Vlad was doing well before his visit. Your
son is a delightful pupil and a good friend
to his classmates. He is doing absolutely
marvellously at school. You'd be very
welcome to come and see what he has been
up to. In fact, you'd be our honoured guests
at the school show – Vlad has the main part,
you know!"

Drax's eyes lit up. "My son on the stage!"

he cried. "Wicked."

Vlad felt warmth flood through him.

"We like a good show, don't we, my evil
one?" Drax said to his wife. "Remember *Bats*?
I took you to see it in Transylvania."

"All right!" Mortemia said, holding up
her hands in defeat. "I can see that I'm
outnumbered here. But you seem to have
forgotten something, Drax," she said to her
husband. "We can't go out in the daylight.
So I'm afraid you'll have to excuse us
from visiting your school," she said to Miss
Lemondrop with a tight smile. "It's one thing
for our son to take stupid risks, but I will not
be putting my life in danger by exposing my
skin to sunlight."

"Have you ever tried?" Miss Lemondrop
asked cautiously. "Only, Lupus and Vlad
seem to be fine outside. I'm sure you could
build up to it gradually."

"We could use this," said Grandpa. He reached into his cape and drew out the tube of sunscreen that Lupus had given him. "They didn't have it in our youth, Mortemia. It seems that humans are quite a few steps ahead of us in their inventions. I've been looking for an opportunity to try it," he added.

"So you've all made up your minds," said Mortemia. "Go ahead. Take Vlad out into the human world. Go to his school and meet his 'friends'," she said. "But don't come crying to me when it all goes wrong and the humans try to lock you up."

Minxie giggled. "You're the one locking up vampires," she pointed out.

Miss Lemondrop smiled and shook her head. "No one is going to lock anyone up," she said.

"But, but humans hate us! You think we

are odd – strange – evil, even!" Mortemia spluttered. "We live differently from you. We go out at night, we change into bats…"

"Things change," Miss Lemondrop said. "Vampires nowadays don't live how they used to, do they? Malika has explained everything to me. In any case, we welcome all sorts of people from different cultures at our school."

"Yeah," Minxie chipped in. "There are people at our school who've come from countries much further away than Transylvania and *their* families do things in different ways and eat different food and wear different clothes. So being a vampire isn't all that special or weird."

"Minxie is right," said Miss Lemondrop.

"But if Vlad starts learning human ways, he'll forget his vampire traditions," said Mortemia despairingly.

"I won't, Mother," said Vlad firmly. "I

want to be a good vampire – I just want
to have friends, too. What's the point
of us staying in this country if we don't
make friends? We might as well move
to Transylvania and only talk to other
vampires."

Minxie stepped forward and put her
hand on Mortemia's arm. The scary vampire
flinched but Minxie didn't pull her hand
away. She looked deep into Mortemia's
bloodshot eyes and said, "What Vlad wants
more than anything is for you to be proud of
him. Please come to the show."

Mortemia pursed her lips.

Everyone waited for her to reply.

"All right," she said eventually. "I will."

Flit flew down and settled on Vlad's
shoulder. "Told you to trust me!" he
squeaked.

The next few weeks went by in a whirlwind for Vlad. It was such a relief not to have to tell fibs and keep secrets any more. He felt as though a huge weight had been lifted off his shoulders. Boz's plan to make everyone frightened of him hadn't worked – instead everyone was on Vlad's side!

When Vlad had gone back to school he had been overwhelmed by how excited everyone was to see him.

Ravi had said he was so jealous that Vlad could turn into a bat. "I wish I could do that.

I'd fly away from my little sister when she's being annoying!"

Of course everyone had had lots of questions, the first one being, "Is it true that vampires suck people's blood?"

Vlad had to answer that question over and over again! He was puzzled about how disappointed his friends were when he told them that he hated the taste.

He had to put his friends right on lots of things – it turned out that they had very old-fashioned ideas of how a vampire behaved.

"Mother might like my school friends if she knew how excited they were about vampire traditions!" Vlad said to Minxie.

The only person who was not thrilled to have a real, live vampire in the school was, of course, Boz. He had tried to bully Vlad on his first day back. He had got him into a corner in the playground.

"You should go back to where you came from," he had snarled. "I told my dad about you. He said that vampires bite humans."

Minxie had come to his rescue. "That's rubbish," she said. "Everyone knows vampires don't bite humans any more."

"They do," Boz had persisted. "If you get bitten by a vampire you turn into a zombie!"

No one had believed him. In the end he gave up bullying Vlad and stayed out of his way.

"I think Boz is actually frightened of you," Minxie told Vlad. "His dad has told him such a load of old rubbish about what vampires are like! Anyway, you should forget all about him now and concentrate on the show."

So that's what Vlad did. He threw himself into the rehearsals and made sure he knew all his lines inside out and back to front. He took his script home and asked Mulch to test him on the words.

The night before the school show, Vlad was having a hot chocolate with the butler in his kitchen.

"I can't wait to come and watch the show," Mulch said, offering Vlad a piece of cake.

Vlad said nothing and didn't take the snack.

"What's the matter, Master Impaler?" Mulch asked.

Vlad looked awkward. He didn't want to offend Mulch. The butler had always been on his side and had been so kind to him – and to Minxie. "It's just that I'm worried about you

coming to watch," Vlad said quietly. "I've only ever acted in front of my friends. What if I can't do it when you and my family are there?"

Mulch's face fell. "We've been looking forward to it so much," he said, his deep voice sounding gloomier than ever. "But if you don't want us to come…"

Vlad felt terrible. Mulch looked so disappointed. "No, it's fine," he said quickly. "Please come. I want you to be there."

When it came to the afternoon of the show, however, Vlad wasn't feeling so brave about his family coming to watch. He waited with Minxie at the side of stage. There was a curtain hiding them from the audience. Some music played while the audience chatted and got settled in their seats.

Vlad peeked round the edge of the curtain. He saw his parents arrive with Grandpa Gory and Mulch. As they walked into the hall, the other people in the audience stopped talking

and everyone turned to look at them.

Vlad fell back into place next to Minxie.
He was shaking.

"They're here!" he whispered to Minxie. "And everyone's staring!"

"Don't worry," said Minxie. "They're just curious. And Mulch is so tall! I don't suppose they've seen anyone that tall before. Besides, everyone's told their parents about your family, so of course people want to get a good look at them. You're famous!"

"I don't want to be famous," said Vlad.

"Well, I think it's brilliant that they're here," said Minxie.

Just then someone turned off the music and Mrs Viola's voice could be heard saying, "Good afternoon, everyone!"

"Shh!" said Minxie before Vlad could say any more.

"Welcome to Badger Class's performance of *Hansel and Gretel*," said Mrs Viola. "I know you're all going to enjoy the show.

Please stay afterwards for tea and biscuits and a chat. I would also like to take this opportunity to say a special hello to a family who are new to the school this term and I know you'll all join me in making them feel welcome. The Impaler family are here tonight to watch their son, Vlad, who will be playing the role of Hansel alongside Malika..."

A murmur went around the audience.

Vlad closed his eyes and gulped.

"Don't be nervous!" Minxie hissed. "You *know* we're going to be great. Everyone loves us as Hansel and Gretel."

Not quite everyone, Vlad thought. He glanced around to see if Boz was anywhere near. He hadn't seen the bully all day. *I hope he's not going to try and ruin things like he did in the auditions*, Vlad thought.

"I feel as though I can't remember any of

my lines," he said aloud.

Minxie rolled her eyes. "Don't be silly. And even if you do, I know your lines, so I can whisper them if you need me to. You don't even have to worry about Boz today, coz he's off sick. And if he comes to watch, Miss Lemondrop and Mr Bendigo will have their eyes on him."

Vlad felt his throat go dry. Mrs Viola had stopped speaking and the murmuring in the audience had died down.

"Ready?" Minxie whispered as Mr Bendigo gave them a signal.

Vlad swallowed. "As I'll ever be," he said.

Mr Bendigo raised the curtain and Minxie and Vlad stepped on to the stage for the opening scene.

Vlad blinked at the bright lights shining down on him. For a second it crossed his mind how far he had come since the first

day he'd walked down the hill from Misery Manor and followed the children into school. Back then he'd been terrified of being frazzled by the sun. He hadn't known anything about human life, other than the things he had read in his *Jollywood Academy* storybook, and he didn't have a friend in the world.

Now he was about to star in the school show, he had learned lots about being a human – as well as perfecting many vampire skills – and he had a best friend. Plus the whole school knew he was a vampire and they didn't care!

Then he spotted his parents, sitting with Grandpa Gory and Mulch in the back row. His father flashed his fangs in a broad smile and Mulch gave him a huge thumbs up.

This is it, Vlad thought. *My chance to show my family something they can be proud of.*

Vlad and Minxie took their places on
the stage as though they were tucked up in
bed, sleeping. Then Ravi and Chitra came
on as the woodcutter father and the wicked
stepmother.

"Look at the children," said Ravi. "They
look so sweet when they are asleep."

Vlad let out a loud Grandpa-Gory-style
snore. "SNOOOAAAARGH!"

Everyone laughed.

Chitra acted as though she were disgusted. "SWEET?" she cried. "They're not sweet! They're a waste of space. I have told you that we can't afford to keep them any longer," she added, wagging her finger at Ravi. "I want you to take them into the forest…" She turned to the audience dramatically and said, "AND LEAVE THEM THERE!"

Everyone booed.

Vlad opened one eye and saw his father,

Mulch and Grandpa Gory booing and joining in with everyone else. His mother was simply glaring at the stage, her arms folded. She didn't look as if she were enjoying the show so far.

The play went on with more children coming on stage dressed as trees. It was time for Vlad and Minxie to pretend to get lost in the forest. As Vlad took the lead through the trees, he realized that one of them was Boz!

Minxie said he was off sick, Vlad thought.

He made himself avoid Boz's eyes and kept walking.

At least he can't do anything to me on stage in front of all these people, Vlad thought.

"Vlad... Vlad!" Minxie was whispering to him. "We're at the witch's house!"

Vlad realized he'd got distracted – it was his turn to speak.

"Look!" he said. "There's a lovely little

cottage. I wonder if the owner will give us something to eat. I'm so hungry."

"Don't bother knocking on the door," said Minxie. "There are sweets and chocolates all over the walls! We can take a few – no one will notice," and she began picking sweets off the model house.

There was a rustling sound from behind Vlad and Minxie and a snigger from the audience.

Vlad whirled round to see Boz-the-tree reach out a "branch" and nick a sweet off the cottage.

The audience laughed.

"Go away," Vlad said between gritted teeth.

"Yum," said Boz-the-tree. "Nice sweeties."

The audience laughed again.

"Use mind control," Minxie whispered.

But before Vlad could do anything, Leisha's witchy voice called out, "What's going on out there? Is there someone outside my cottage?"

"Yes," said Boz-the-tree. "Two little children who are stealing your sweets."

Minxie glared at Boz, but he didn't care. The audience was laughing and Boz was looking triumphant. Everyone was enjoying Boz's interruptions – they thought it was part of the show!

Leisha came out of the house and looked shocked when she saw Boz-the-tree standing next to Vlad and Minxie.

"What's that tree doing there?" she asked.

The audience laughed again.

Vlad was starting to feel desperate. He couldn't think what to do or say! Boz was ruining everything again. If he didn't shut up soon, Vlad's parents would think that Boz was the star of the show and that Vlad had been lying about having the lead role. He stared at Boz, open-mouthed.

"If you don't do something, I will!" said Minxie, under the laughter from the crowd.

She took a step towards Boz but he was too quick for her. He stuck out one of his "branches" and sent poor Minxie flying into the cottage, which crashed to the ground!

Minxie lay on top of the broken model house and her face collapsed.

Vlad realized with horror that she was going to cry. The school bully was ruining the show and he, Vlad, was doing nothing to stop it.

There was a gasp in the audience and Mrs Viola and Mr Bendigo began making their way towards the stage. A loud murmur had started up as everyone realized that the play was not going to plan.

Minxie picked herself up and Vlad made a move towards her to see if she was OK. But Boz stepped in front of Vlad and said, "What're you going to do now, Vampire Boy? Use your magic powers to make everything all right?"

Something inside Vlad snapped.

"Yes!" he cried. He took hold of Boz around the trunk part of his costume and lifted him clean off the ground!

Mrs Viola and Mr Bendigo stopped in their tracks and stared as Vlad carried Boz off the stage.

"PUT ME DOWN!" Boz yelled. "PUT ME DOWN!"

"A woodcutter's son knows how to get rid of unwanted trees," said Minxie loudly, as Vlad and Boz left the stage. A cheer went up from the back of the hall and the rest of the audience joined in.

The play went on as planned after Boz had gone. The audience laughed and cheered and clapped in all the right places. Vlad had never enjoyed himself so much in his life. Afterwards he took Minxie to find his parents.

"Wasn't he great?" said Minxie loyally.

"He was!" said Mulch. "And so were you."

"Thanks," said Minxie, blushing. "I couldn't have done it without Vlad though –

he saved me from that stupid tree!"

Mulch gave a booming laugh.

"Yes, well done, my little devil!" cried
Drax, slapping Vlad on the back. "You were
wicked!"

"Marvellous acting," Grandpa Gory
agreed.

Vlad felt his face go hot with pleasure.
"Thank you," he said, beaming.

"And these biscuits are delicious,"
Grandpa muttered, taking a handful from the
plate Miss Lemondrop was passing around.

Vlad was looking anxiously at his mother.
"Did you like the show?" he asked.

"Hmm, you were quite impressive," said
Mortemia grudgingly. "And I'm pleased to
see you've mastered super-strength at last,
too. Came in handy after all, didn't it?" she
said to Drax.

"Yes, dear," said Drax, winking at Vlad.

149

"Vampire skills still have their place. So would you say that Vlad is a proper vampire now, my little blood cell?" he asked Mortemia.

"Yes," said Vlad's mother. And she smiled!

Vlad was so shocked he didn't know what to say.

"He's the world's *best* vampire!" Minxie cried, punching the air.

Vlad beamed. "And you're the world's best vampire's best friend!" he said.

"I'll drink to that!" said Grandpa Gory, raising his cup of tea. "Mwahahahahaha!"

Encyclopedia

of Curious

Creatures

Fairy
(Also: faerie)
A tiny creature that looks like a human, but has wings. Can perform magic. Is often mischievous and enjoys playing tricks.

Ghost
(from Old English: *gāst*, 'spirit')
Spirit of a dead person or animal. Often appears white or see-through. Can walk through walls. Makes spooky sounds, such as "Whoooo!" Sometimes haunts old houses or graveyards.

Giant
(from Latin and Greek: *gigas*, 'giant')
A huge creature that looks like a human. Extremely strong. Likes to fight.

Mermaid

(from Old English: *mere* + maid, 'sea girl')
A sea creature with the head and upper body of a girl and the tail of a fish. Often seen during storms and shipwrecks.

Werewolf

(from Old English: *werwulf*, 'man wolf')
A human who is able to turn into a wolf after he or she has been bitten by a wolf. Transformation happens by the light of the moon.

Witch

(from Old English: *wicca* or *wicce*, 'witch')
A person (usually an old woman) who can do magic. Often makes potions from frogs' legs and newts' eyes. Sometimes has green skin. Wears mostly black and is often seen with a black cat. Can travel on a broomstick.

Collect them all!

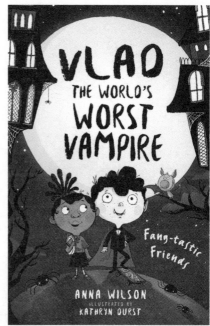

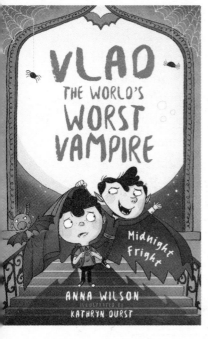

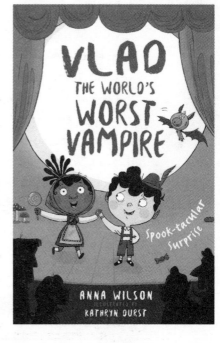

Anna Wilson LOVES stories. She has
been a bookworm since she could first hold a
book and always knew she wanted a job that
involved writing or reading or both. She has
written picture books, short stories, poems
and young fiction series including *Nina Fairy
Ballerina*, *Top of the Pups*, *The Pooch Parlour* and
Kitten Chaos. Anna lives with her family in
Bradford-on-Avon, Wiltshire.

www.annawilson.co.uk

Kathryn has a passion for illustration, design, animation, film and puppetry! She attended Sheridan College for the Bachelor of Applied Arts – 2D Animation Program and completed an internship at Pixar Animation Studios for storyboarding. She loves working on children's entertainment, publications and media – especially kids' books – and television series. She is currently based in Toronto, Canada.

www.kathryndurst.com

"[AN] ENTERTAININGLY BATTY AND
WONDERFULLY WITTY SERIES."

LANCASHIRE EVENING POST

"DELIGHTFULLY ILLUSTRATED ... AN ENGAGING
STORY ABOUT A CUTE CHARACTER WHO KNOWS
JUST WHAT HE WANTS FROM LIFE."

PARENTS IN TOUCH

"WARM AND FUNNY."

FLEUR HITCHCOCK, AUTHOR